This book belongs to

....

www.usborne.com
First published in 2006 by Usborne Publishing Ltd.,
Usborne House, 83-85 Saffron Hill, London ECIN 8RT, England. Copyright © 2006 Usborne Publishing Ltd.

Usborne
Farmyard Tales Treasury

Illustrated by
Stephen Cartwright

Edited by Minna Lacey
Designed by Michelle Lawrence

Stories by Heather Amery
Projects by Anna Milbourne
Songs arranged by Anthony Marks

Can you find the little yellow duck on every double page?

Contents

Stories from Apple Tree Farm

Farmyard Tales things to make and do

Farmyard Tales songs and rhymes

This is Apple Tree Farm

Mr. and Mrs. Boot live here with their two children, Poppy and Sam. They have a dog called Rusty and a cat called Whiskers.

This is Ted. Ted works at Apple Tree Farm. He drives the tractor and looks after all the other farm machines. He is always busy mending things.

Who's who at Apple Tree Farm

Mrs. Boot

Mr. Boot

Ted

Rusty the dog

Sam

Poppy

Woolly the sheep

Fluff the kitten

Curly the piglet

Whiskers the cat

Dolly the carthorse

Ears the donkey

Pippin the pony

Daisy the cow

Gertie the goat

A day at the farm

Poppy and Sam are up early in the morning to help Mrs. Boot feed the animals and do all the jobs that need to be done. Rusty wants to help too.

At 9 o'clock Sam empties out a bucket of food for the pigs.

Poppy gives Pippin the pony a bundle of fresh hay at 10 o'clock.

At 11 o'clock, Poppy and Sam help fill up the sheep's trough.

Lunch is at 1 o'clock. Mrs. Boot has made a delicious picnic.

Poppy and Sam help bring the cows in to be milked at 4 o'clock.

After a tiring day, at 7 o'clock Sam and Poppy are ready to go to bed.

Stories from Apple Tree Farm

Pig Gets Stuck

At Apple Tree Farm there is a big mother pig and five baby pigs. The smallest pig is called Curly. Like all pigs, he has a curly tail. The pigs live in a pen with a little pigsty.

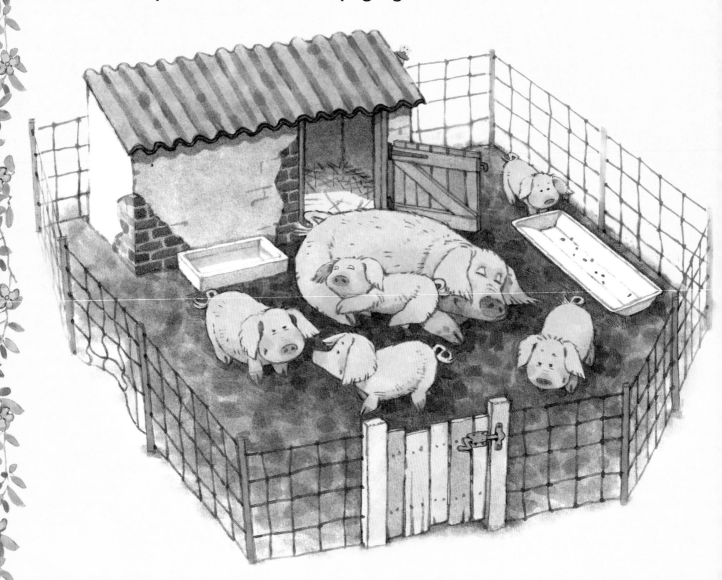

Every morning Mrs. Boot carries a big bucket of
breakfast to the pigs. They always crowd around
the trough, pushing their snouts into the food.
But, this morning, Curly can't squeeze in between
his big brothers and sisters.

Curly has no breakfast, so he is very hungry and
miserable. He wanders around the pen, snuffling
for something to eat. But he can't find anything.

Then he sees a gap under the fence, just big enough for him to crawl through. Feeling a bit scared at being by himself, Curly trots off across the farmyard, looking for something to eat.

First he comes to the cows who are very busy munching their breakfast. Curly wonders what they are eating. He sniffs it. It's only hay. He doesn't like hay. It's much too dry and dull. He wants to find something more tasty.

Curly leaves the cows and scampers on until he comes to the sheep. They are chewing away at hay, too. Nothing there for me, thinks Curly.

Next he squeezes under the fence into a big field. There he stops to look at the horse, but the horse is eating hay too. Curly is puzzled. Doesn't anyone eat anything but hay for breakfast?

Curly trots off to where the geese are nibbling at the grass. One big goose stares and hisses at him. He quickly decides it's time to move on.

Next, Curly finds a fence and peeks through a gap. Inside are lots of hens. They have a big bowl of food and it looks good to Curly.

He puts his head through the fence. The gap might just be big enough for him to squeeze through. Scrabbling on the ground, he pushes himself into the hen run. It is a very tight fit.

Curly puts his snout into the hens' bowl and takes a mouthful of their food. It tastes delicious to a very hungry pig. Grunting, he begins to eat.

The hens squawk at Curly, but he is too busy eating to take any notice. Soon there is no food left. Curly feels very full and very happy. But the hens are not so happy.

Suddenly he hears a shout. He looks up. There is Mrs. Boot, leaning over the fence.

"What are you doing in the hen run, Curly?" she shouts. "How did you get in there, you naughty little pig?"

Mrs. Boot looks very cross. Curly is scared. He quickly scampers off to the gap in the fence.

He tries to push his head through but then he is stuck. His body won't follow. He has eaten so much of the hens' food, his tummy is far too fat to go through the fence.

Curly pushes and pushes. He tries to squeeze through, but he can't move. He squeals louder and louder. Poppy, Sam and Rusty come running to see what all the noise is about.

"Curly looks so funny," says Poppy, laughing.

Mrs. Boot lifts Curly up and tries to push him through the fence.

"Poppy and Sam," says Mrs. Boot, "help me to push him through."

Mrs. Boot pushes, Poppy pushes and Sam pushes, but the little pig is well and truly stuck.

Suddenly, Curly grunts very loudly, gives a very big wriggle, and pops through the gap in the fence.

"He's out, he's out," shouts Sam. Curly lies on the ground, too tired to get to his feet and run away.

"Poor little thing," says Poppy.

Mrs. Boot picks him up and holds him gently in her arms.

"He's all right now," she says and she carries him back to the pig sty.

"I think little Curly was just hungry. Tomorrow I'll make sure he gets plenty of breakfast."

And from then on, Curly never, ever went hungry again or had to go looking for his breakfast.

Scarecrow's Secret

One Saturday morning, Poppy and Sam go out to play with Rusty. They soon find Mr. Boot working away in the barn. He is tying lots of straw around a big wooden pole.

"What are you making, Dad?" asks Sam.

"It looks very funny. What is it?" says Poppy.

"You'll soon see," says Mr. Boot.

The children still can't guess what he is making.
"Now," says Mr. Boot, "would you please go and get my old coat. It's in the shed. And bring my old hat as well."

A few minutes later, they come back with the old coat and hat. Mr. Boot has put a sack on the top of the pole and made a face on it.

"Now I know what it is," shouts Poppy. "It's a scarecrow!" She and Sam help Mr. Boot to put the coat on the scarecrow.

Then they put the old hat on his head and tie a
scarf around his neck.

"Here are some gloves for him," says Sam.

"He looks just like a very nice old man," says
Poppy. "I'm going to call him Mr. Straw."

Whiskers, the cat, watches what is going on and
sniffs at the scarecrow.

"There, he's finished now," says Mr. Boot,
"and ready to start work. Poppy, you take one
end and help me carry him out to the field. He's
not very heavy. And, please, Sam, bring the
shovel. We'll need that."

Poppy and Mr. Boot carry Mr. Straw to a field that has been sown with wheat. Mr. Boot digs a big hole in the ground and pushes the pole into it, so that Mr. Straw stands up straight.

"He looks almost like a real man," says Poppy.
"I'm sure he'll scare off all the birds," adds Sam, "especially the crows."
"We'll leave Mr. Straw now so he can get on with the scaring," says Mr. Boot.

Next morning, Poppy, Sam and Mr. Boot walk out to the wheat field to look at Mr. Straw.

"He's a very good scarecrow. There are no birds in this field," says Poppy.

They walk along to Farmer Dray's field.

"Look at Farmer Dray's scarecrow," says Mr. Boot. "He's not scaring the birds away at all."

Every day, Poppy, Sam and Rusty go to look at their scarecrow. One morning, Sam says,

"Why do you think Mr. Straw is so good at scaring the birds?"

"I don't know," says Poppy, "but sometimes I think he looks as if he's moving. His coat goes up and down. It's very strange."

"Let's go and have a closer look," says Sam.

"Come on, Rusty," says Poppy.

Poppy, Sam and Rusty climb very quietly through the fence and creep across the field towards Mr. Straw.

They walk around Mr. Straw, looking at him very carefully. Rusty sniffs at him but doesn't bark.

"Look, Sam, I think there's something inside his coat, and it's moving," whispers Poppy. "It's making a funny little squeaky noise."

"Let's look inside," says Sam. Poppy undoes a button and gently pulls open Mr. Straw's coat.

"It's Whiskers," whispers Sam.

"And two baby kittens, hiding in the straw," says Poppy. "Aren't they lovely?"

Sam and Poppy take out the kittens from Mr. Straw's coat and stroke them. Whiskers watches, looking very proud.

"That's our scarecrow's secret," says Poppy.

"Mr. Straw has Whiskers to help him to frighten the birds."

"Clever Whiskers and clever Mr. Straw," says Sam, and they carefully put the kittens back inside Mr. Straw's coat.

The Naughty Sheep

Mrs. Boot keeps seven white sheep at Apple Tree Farm. They live in a big field with a fence all around it, and a gate that is usually kept firmly shut. One of the sheep has a black patch over one eye. She is called Woolly.

One morning, Woolly looks through the fence. She is bored of eating grass and wishes she could find something more interesting to eat.

She trots around the field, trying to find a way out. Then she notices that the gate isn't quite shut. She pushes with her nose and opens the gate a little wider. With another push, the gate opens just wide enough for her to squeeze through.

Woolly scampers across the farmyard. Then she sees another gate. This one is wide open. She walks through it and looks around. She is in Mrs. Boot's garden and it is full of flowers. She nibbles at a few. They are so pretty and taste so much better than boring old green grass.

34

Woolly runs around tasting lots of other flowers.
She knocks over a flowerpot, but she doesn't care.
Woolly thinks the flowers are scrumptious. She's
never had such a feast. Suddenly she hiccups.
Perhaps garden flowers are not the best things for
a sheep to eat after all.

Then Woolly hears a noise and stops chewing. "What are you doing in my garden, Woolly?" shouts Mrs. Boot, looking over the fence. "You've eaten my flowers. Come out at once. You're a very, very naughty sheep."

Mrs. Boot is very angry.

"It's the village show today," she says to Poppy and Sam. "I was going to pick my best flowers for it. I thought I might win a prize this year. But look at them now. Woolly has ruined them."

Woolly is scared and runs out of the garden. She hides behind the fence and watches Mrs. Boot and the children hurry away. She knows she has done something really naughty.

"Come on," says Mrs. Boot, "we're going to be late. The show will have started by the time we get there."

Mrs. Boot, Poppy, Sam and, of course, Rusty run down the lane to Apple Tree Village. This is where the show is held each year. Woolly watches them go. They haven't taken her back to the sheep field, so she starts to follow them.

Woolly soon comes to the big field in the village where the show is held. She stops at the entrance and looks around. All she can see is the backs of lots of people. They are all watching something and clapping. She can't see Mrs. Boot, Poppy, Sam or Rusty anywhere.

Farm Show

She pushes through the legs of the crowd, ducks under a rope and stops in a big open square of grass. Two other sheep are standing beside a man in a white coat. Woolly doesn't know what to do. Everyone seems to be staring at her and talking very loudly.

Suddenly Mrs. Boot comes running up to her.
"How did you get here?" asks Mrs. Boot.
"You're supposed to be back at Apple Tree Farm."

"Well, whatever she's doing, she's just won a
prize for the best sheep in the show,"
says the man. "Here's a
silver cup for you
and a badge for
your sheep."

"That's wonderful," says Mrs. Boot, laughing. "Thank you very much."

When the show is finally over, Mrs. Boot, Poppy, Sam and Rusty take Woolly back to Apple Tree Farm. Mrs. Boot carries the silver cup and Woolly wears the badge.

She knows something good has happened and looks very pleased with herself.

"Come on, Woolly," says Mrs. Boot, "you're going back to your field now and you're not to get out again. You're a very naughty, but very clever sheep."

The Runaway Tractor

Ted looks after the farm machines and drives the tractor at Apple Tree Farm. Poppy and Sam often go and look for Ted. He is always up to something.

One morning, Ted loads the trailer with hay and drives off to the field to feed the sheep. Poppy and Sam watch him go.

Poppy and Sam run off to play in the barn. Suddenly Sam says, "Listen, Ted is shouting and the tractor is making a funny noise."

"Let's go and look," says Poppy. They run up the hill and see the tractor racing down the other side.

"I don't know what's happened. I can't make the tractor stop," shouts Ted.

The tractor races on. Then the trailer comes off the tractor. It tears down the hill and smashes into the fence with a great crash. The trailer tips up and spills out all the hay. Poppy, Sam and Rusty run down the hill after the tractor.

The tractor goes straight through the fence. Ted clings to the steering wheel as the tractor roars on, down the hill and into the pond. It makes a huge splash, frightening off the ducks which fly up into the air, quacking loudly.

The tractor engine coughs and splutters, and then finally stops with a loud hiss. Suddenly it's all very quiet.

"Oh, dear," says Poppy.

"Are you all right, Ted?" shouts Sam.

"I'm fine," says Ted. "But the tractor's not. I thought it would never stop."

Ted climbs down from the tractor, which has little puffs of steam coming out of it. He wades out of the pond. The water is so deep it creeps over the top of his boots. Poppy, Sam and Rusty run to the pond to see if they can help.

Poor Ted is very wet. He pulls off his boots, one at a time, and tips out the water. Poppy holds him up while he stands on one foot, and then the other.

"How are you going to get the tractor out of the pond?" asks Poppy.

"We'll have to ask Farmer Dray for some help," says Ted, wringing out his wet socks. "Poppy and Sam, please can you ask your mother to telephone Farmer Dray."

Poppy, Sam and Rusty run off to the farmhouse.

Cold and wet, Ted waits by the pond in the field. Soon Poppy, Sam and Rusty return with Farmer Dray, from the farm next door. Farmer Dray is leading Dolly, his carthorse.

"I love Dolly," says Poppy. "She's so friendly."

"Don't worry, Ted," says Farmer Dray. "We'll soon have the tractor out of there."

Farmer Dray has two strong ropes with him. He ties one end of each rope to Dolly's harness. Ted ties the other ends to the front of the tractor.

Dolly leans on the ropes and takes a few steps forwards, pulling very hard. Very slowly, the tractor begins to move a little, then stops. Ted starts pushing, while Dolly pulls.

"Come on, old girl," says Farmer Dray. "Show us what you can do."

Suddenly, as Dolly pulls harder, the tractor leaps forward with a jerk, taking everyone by surprise. Ted loses his grip and falls over into the pond.

Now he's wet and muddy all over, and his boots are full of water again. Ted doesn't look very happy. With a few more strong pulls from Dolly, the tractor comes out of the pond.

"Better leave it to dry out. You can come back later to get the engine started," says Farmer Dray.

"Ted, you're all wet," cries Sam.

"And muddy," says Poppy, trying not to laugh.

Farmer Dray picks up Poppy and Sam, and puts them on Dolly's back. Then he climbs up too.

"Off home, now. Hold on tight," he says, as Dolly plods along.

"Well done, Dolly," says Sam.

"Isn't this exciting?" says Poppy. Ted is so wet he has to walk in his wet boots.

"Thanks very much for your help," he says to Farmer Dray, and sneezes twice.

The Grumpy Goat

One morning, Mrs. Boot, Poppy, Sam and Rusty are coming back from the orchard where they have been picking apples. On the way back home, they see Ted pushing a wheelbarrow full of straw.

"Where are you going?" asks Mrs. Boot.

"I'm taking the straw to the goat shed," says Ted. "I was looking for you, Poppy and Sam. It's your turn to clean the goat shed."

Poppy and Sam go with Ted, as he pushes his wheelbarrow, to find Gertie the goat.

"Will she let us clean her shed?" asks Sam. "She looks very grumpy."

"Take no notice of her," says Ted.

Poppy and Sam open the gate and hurry to the shed. Gertie trots straight up to Sam and butts him.

"Quick, run before she does it again," calls Poppy.

The children run out of
the field and shut
the gate.

"We'll have to get
Gertie out of this
field to clean her
shed," says Poppy,
"but I don't know
how we'll do it."

"I've got an idea," says Sam. He walks away to
the farmhouse and returns with a bag of bread.
"Here, Gertie," he says, "some bread for you."

Gertie eats the bread and the bag, but doesn't move out of her pen.

"Let's try some grass," says Poppy. She pulls up a big bunch and leaves it by the gate. Gertie gobbles up the grass, then trots back into her pen.

"I've got another idea," says Sam.

"What's that?" asks Poppy.

"Gertie never butts Ted. If I looked like Ted, she wouldn't butt me, would she?" says Sam.

"But you don't look at all like Ted," says Poppy.

"Wait and see," says Sam, and he hurries back to the farmhouse.

Sam soon comes back wearing Ted's old coat
and hat. He strides into the field and tries to look
tall, like Ted. Gertie trots straight
up to him and butts him.

"I know, I'll get a
rope," says Poppy,
and she soon
comes back with
one. She whirls
the rope around
and throws it at
Gertie. She misses.

"Run!" shouts Sam, "she's going to butt me again." They all run out and Gertie follows them. "She's out," shouts Sam. "Quick, shut the gate." Gertie trots away into the outside field. Quickly Poppy and Sam start cleaning out Gertie's shed.

They sweep up all the old straw and spread fresh straw over the shed floor.

"Come on, Gertie," calls Sam. "You can come back now."

Poppy and Sam stand behind the gate so she can't butt them. She trots past, then glares at them.

"You are a grumpy old goat, Gertie," says Poppy.

"We've cleaned out your shed and given you fresh straw, and you're still grumpy," says Sam.

"Come on," says Poppy, "we'll leave her to be grumpy on her own."

They walk back to the farmhouse.

Next morning, Ted comes to find Poppy and Sam.
"Have you seen Gertie today?" he says.

"No," says Poppy, "I'm not going near her. She's too grumpy."

"Well, come over and have a look," says Ted.

In the field with Gertie is a tiny goat, just able to stand on its wobbly legs.

"Gertie gave birth to a kid last night," says Ted.

"She doesn't look so grumpy now," says Sam, "but I'm not going in her field, just in case."

Camping Out

It is a hot, sunny summer afternoon. Mrs. Boot is busy cutting the grass. Sam rakes up the grass for her and helps Poppy put it in the wheelbarrow. Suddenly, they hear a car stop at the gate.

"I wonder who that is," says Mrs. Boot.

"Let's go and see," says Sam.

Mrs. Boot, Poppy and Sam walk to the gate and open it. A man, a woman and a boy get out of a car.

"Hello," says the man. "We're on a camping trip.

May we put up our tent in a field on your farm, please?"

"Yes, of course. You can camp in that field over there," says Mrs. Boot. "We'll show you the way."

The campers start unloading their car and put up their big tent. Poppy and Sam help them. They carry chairs, a table, a cooking stove and food out of the car and put the things down on the grass outside the tent.

Then they all walk back to the farmhouse. Mrs. Boot hands the campers a bucket of water and a jug of fresh milk. Poppy runs into the kitchen and comes out with a basket of eggs.

"Dad," asks Sam, "can we go camping too?"

"All right," says Mr. Boot, and he goes off to find the tent.

Poppy and Sam carry the tent to the field. They sort out the poles, ropes, tent pegs and cover, and start trying to put up the tent. They put on the cover, but the tent keeps falling down. Rusty is very excited and tries to push his way in.

"Come out of there, Rusty," shouts Sam.

They pick up the tent cover and start again. They push and pull, shouting at each other and at Rusty. At last, the tent is firmly up.

Mrs. Boot walks out to the field.

"Poppy and Sam, come and have supper," she calls. "You can come back to the tent after supper, but you must brush your teeth first."

"Your tent looks good," says the man, who is standing nearby.

After supper, when they're ready for bed, Poppy and Sam walk across the yard to their tent.

"Come on, Rusty, you can come too," says Sam. They crawl into the tent and tie up the door flaps. Then they wriggle into their sleeping bags.

"Isn't camping fun?" giggles Poppy.

"Rusty, stop playing. It's time for bed," says Poppy. They start to go to sleep. Suddenly, Sam sits up.

"Poppy, wake up," he whispers. "What's that noise? There's something walking around the tent."

Poppy sits up and listens.

"I don't know," she whispers back. "I'll have a look outside."

Poppy scrambles out of her sleeping bag, opens the tent flap and looks outside.

"Can you see anything?" asks Sam.

"It's only old Daisy, the cow," she says. "She must have come in from the next field."

Poppy closes the tent flap and climbs into her sleeping bag again.

"Lie down and go to sleep, Rusty," she says.

Then the door flap bulges in and Daisy pushes her big head into the tent.

"Go away, Daisy," shouts Poppy.

Rusty jumps up and barks. Daisy tries to back out, but the tent flaps catch on her ears.

Daisy pulls the tent down and runs away with it wrapped around her. Rusty chases after her.

"What shall we do now?" asks Sam.

"We can't camp without a tent," says Poppy. "We'll have to go back to the house."

Mr. Boot hears Daisy mooing and opens the door of the farmhouse.

"Hello, Dad. We've come back because Daisy's run off with our tent," says Sam.

"I'd better go and get it off her while you go upstairs to bed," says Mr. Boot.

"I love camping," says Poppy. "It's so exciting."

Farmyard Tales
things to
make and do

Cut-out farm animals

1. Fold a rectangle of thick white paper in half, with the two shorter edges together. Then, press firmly along the fold.

2. Draw a straight line a finger's width from the bottom. Fold the paper inward along the line. Do the same on the other side.

3. Draw a cow on the folded paper, like this. Make its back go along the top fold and its feet go to the bottom.

Don't cut along this side.

Don't cut here.

4. Cut out the cow shape, cutting through both sides of the folded paper. Don't cut along its back or the bottom of its feet.

5. Turn the folded paper over and draw the cow on the blank side too. Fill it in on both sides of the paper using felt-tip pens.

6. Cut out a small rectangle of thick green paper. Spread glue onto the folds under the cow's feet and press them onto the green paper.

You can make more animals in the same way, to create your own farmyard.

71

Carrot print robins

Wash
the spoon
between
spreading each
different paint.

Throw this ——
piece away.

1. Fold three kitchen
paper towels and lay
them on top of a pile
of old newspapers.

2. Pour brown, red and
white paint onto the paper
towels. Spread the paint
with the back of a spoon.

3. Cut a big carrot into
four pieces. You don't
need to keep the second
smallest piece.

4. Press the thickest piece
of carrot into the brown
paint. Press it onto paper
to print a robin's body.

5. Press the piece of carrot
into the paint again and
print another body. Do
this a few more times.

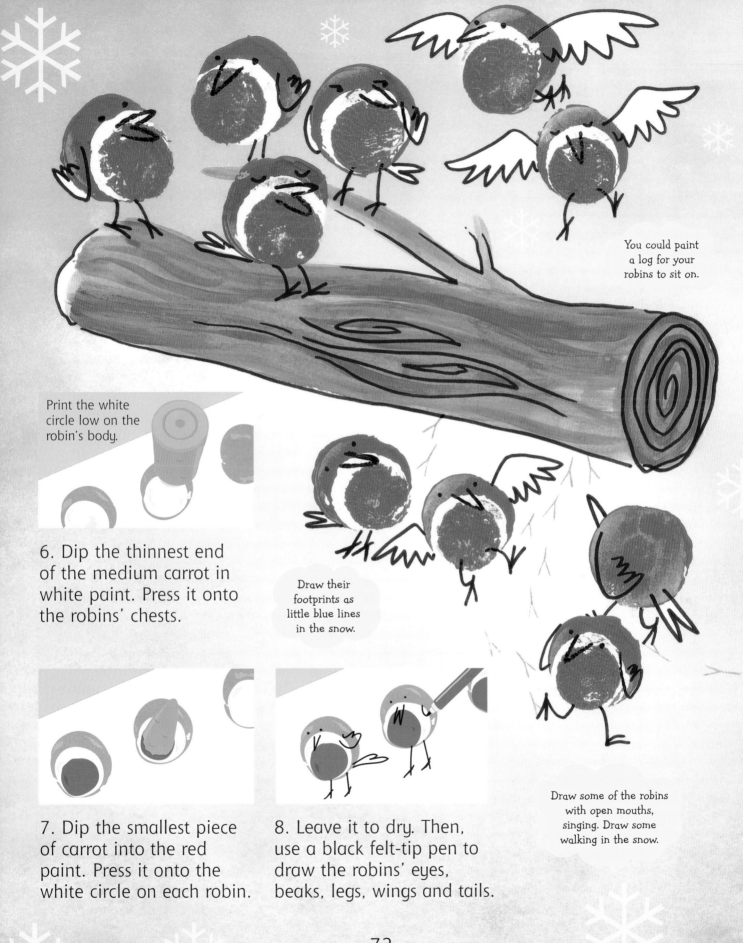

You could paint a log for your robins to sit on.

Print the white circle low on the robin's body.

6. Dip the thinnest end of the medium carrot in white paint. Press it onto the robins' chests.

Draw their footprints as little blue lines in the snow.

7. Dip the smallest piece of carrot into the red paint. Press it onto the white circle on each robin.

8. Leave it to dry. Then, use a black felt-tip pen to draw the robins' eyes, beaks, legs, wings and tails.

Draw some of the robins with open mouths, singing. Draw some walking in the snow.

Piggy picture frame

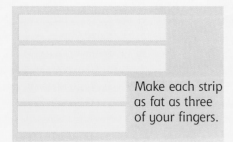

Make each strip as fat as three of your fingers.

1. Cut two strips of thick yellow paper about the length of this page and two more strips about the width of this page.

2. Spread glue on both ends of one of the short strips. Press the long strips onto it. Glue on the other short strip to make a frame.

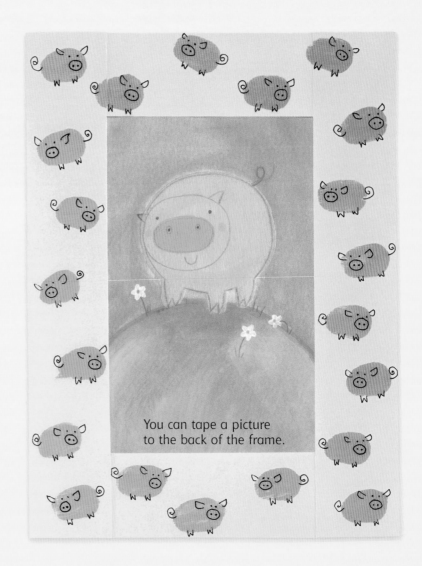

You can tape a picture to the back of the frame.

If you don't have pink paint, mix some white and red paint together.

3. Pour a little pink paint onto a plate. Dip your finger into the paint. Press it onto the frame to print a pig's body. Print lots more.

4. Let the paint dry. Then, use a black felt-tip pen to draw the pigs' eyes, ears and snouts. Add legs and give each one a curly tail.

Pussycat bookmark

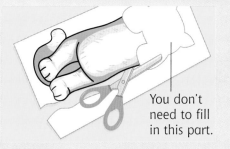

You don't need to fill in this part.

1. On a piece of thick white paper, draw a cat's head and two paws, like this. Then, fill them in with felt-tip pens.

2. Cut carefully around the cat shape. Then, put it on top of another piece of thick paper and draw around it using a pencil.

3. Add the cat's body under the pencil outline and fill it in with felt-tip pens. Then, cut around the whole cat shape.

Hook the cat's paws over a page to mark your place in a book.

4. Spread glue on the top part of the cat's head. Then, press the filled-in head shape on top, making sure the ears line up.

Growing shoots

If you don't have any beans, you can use dried chickpeas instead.

1. Put four dried beans into a small bowl. Pour water on top to cover them. Then, leave them to soak for half an hour.

2. Soak an old jar in warm, soapy water and peel off the labels. Then, rinse the jar well with cold water. Leave it wet on the inside.

It takes about two weeks for beans and chickpeas to grow into shoots like these.

You could decorate your jar using a strip of green paper, with cut-out paper flowers on top.

When your shoot starts to grow over the top of the jar, it's big enough to plant in soil.

3. Scrunch up a paper towel. Open out a bright paper napkin and wrap it around the scrunched-up paper towel to make a bundle.

4. Push the bundle into the jar. Hold the napkin away from the side of the jar and push a bean down between the jar and the napkin.

5. Push the other three beans between the napkin and the side of the jar. Then, press the napkin back to hold them in place.

6. Use a big spoon to add water to the jar, making sure the napkin gets fairly wet. Then, put the jar in a warm, bright place.

Planting your shoot

7. Spoon more water into the jar every day, to keep the napkin wet. After two or three days, some shoots will begin to grow.

Make the dip big enough to hold your shoot's roots.

1. Put some small stones into a plant pot with a hole in it. Fill the pot almost to the top with compost. Make a dip in the compost.

Let the roots sit in the dip.

2. Lift a shoot out of the jar. Hold it upright in the pot and add compost around it. Press the compost down. Water it every few days.

Pretty eggs

Cooking the eggs

To make six pretty eggs, you will need:

6 eggs, at room temperature
food dye
wax crayons
tiny star-shaped stickers
rubber bands

1. Put the eggs into a pan of cold water. Heat the pan until the water is gently boiling, then reduce the heat a little.

Use a slotted spoon.

2. Cook the eggs for eight to nine minutes. Lift out one egg at a time. Cool them in a bowl of cold water for ten minutes.

The wax resists the food dye.

1. Using a wax crayon, draw patterns on a dry egg. Then, add 3-4 teaspoons of bright food dye into a glass.

Leave the egg for about ten minutes.

2. Half fill the glass with water, then put the egg into the glass. Using a spoon, turn the egg until it is covered with the dye.

3. When the egg is bright enough, lift it out of the glass with a spoon. Then, place it on a paper towel to dry completely.

Stickers

Make sure the egg is dry.

1. Press tiny stickers all over another egg. Use shiny ones if you can, because they don't soak up so much food dye.

2. Put the egg in a glass of food dye, as you did before. Then, lift the egg out with a spoon and put it on a paper towel to dry.

3. When the egg is completely dry, carefully peel off the stickers. You'll see pale shapes where the stickers were before.

The eggs need to be stored in a refrigerator and eaten within three days.

You could eat them with a fresh mixed salad or on their own.

Stripes

1. Stretch a short, thick rubber band around another dry egg. Then, stretch one around the egg from the top to the bottom.

2. Add lots more rubber bands, then dye the egg and let it dry. Then, remove the rubber bands to see stripes of eggshell.

79

Apple picking puzzle

Can you find these things in the picture?

apple   tree   bird   hen   bee

leaf   kitten   ladder   fox   flower

caterpillar   swing   snail   beetle

By the stream puzzle

Can you find these
things in the picture?

fish

frog

bridge

pond

jar

haystack

scarecrow

boat

rabbit

tent

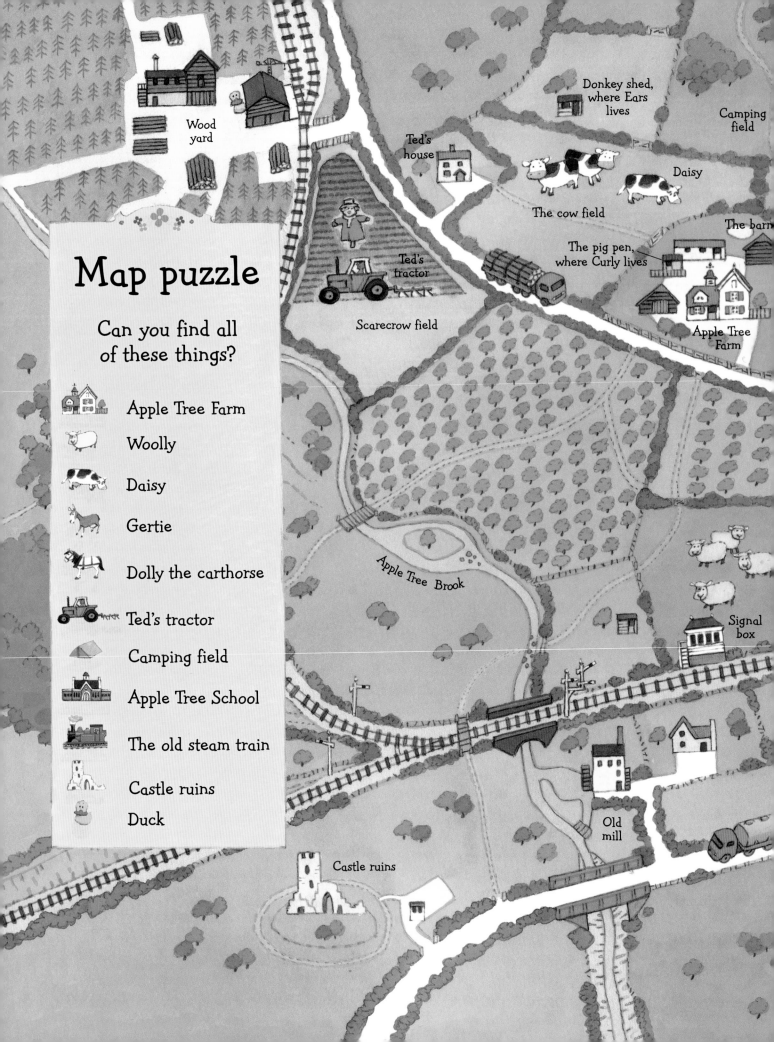

Wood yard

Donkey shed, where Ears lives

Camping field

Ted's house

Daisy

The cow field

The barn

The pig pen, where Curly lives

Apple Tree Farm

Ted's tractor

Scarecrow field

Map puzzle

Can you find all of these things?

- Apple Tree Farm
- Woolly
- Daisy
- Gertie
- Dolly the carthorse
- Ted's tractor
- Camping field
- Apple Tree School
- The old steam train
- Castle ruins
- Duck

Apple Tree Brook

Signal box

Old mill

Castle ruins

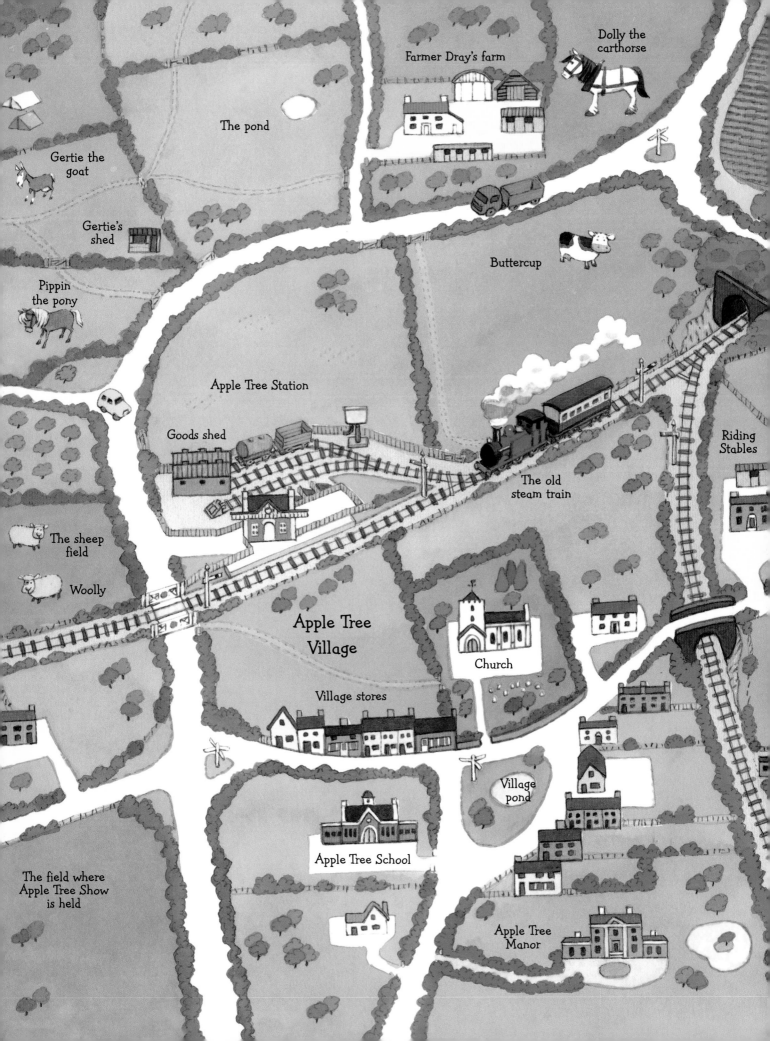

Dolly the carthorse

Farmer Dray's farm

The pond

Gertie the goat

Gertie's shed

Buttercup

Pippin the pony

Apple Tree Station

Goods shed

The old steam train

Riding Stables

The sheep field

Woolly

Apple Tree Village

Church

Village stores

Village pond

Apple Tree School

The field where Apple Tree Show is held

Apple Tree Manor

Farmyard Tales songs and rhymes

Where has our little pig gone?

(to the tune of "Where has my little dog gone?")

Where, oh where has our little pig gone?
Oh where, oh where can he be?
He's not in the cowshed, he's not in the barn,
Oh where, oh where can he be?

88

Sam's little kitten

(to the tune of "Pussycat, pussycat")

Sam's little kitten has gone for a ride,
Off went the truck with her hiding inside!
Now we'll go searching with Ted in the car,
I do hope that Fluff hasn't gone very far!

Now we are home at the end of the day,
We still haven't found her, has she run away?
Here's Mister Bran, he's got Fluff in his arms,
Now she is safe back at Apple Tree Farm.

89

Poppy put the kettle on

(to the tune of "Polly put the kettle on")

Poppy put the kettle on,
Poppy put the kettle on,
Poppy put the kettle on,
We'll all have tea!

Mrs. Boot has made a cake,
Mrs. Boot has made a cake,
Mrs. Boot has made a cake,
For us to eat.

To listen to the tune of this song, go to the Usborne Quicklinks Website
at **www.usborne-quicklinks.com** and type the keywords "treasury songs".

Pat-a-cake, pat-a-cake

(to the traditional tune)

Pat-a-cake, pat-a-cake, baker's man,

    (Clap your hands.)

Bake me a cake just as fast as you can!

    (Rub your hands together.)

Pat it and prick it and mark it with "P"

    (Use a finger to trace the letter "P" on your palm.)

And put it in the oven for Poppy and me.

    (Pretend you are eating a cake.)

To listen to the tune of this song, go to the Usborne Quicklinks Website at **www.usborne-quicklinks.com** and type the keywords "treasury songs".

Woolly had a little lamb

(to the tune of "Mary had a little lamb")

Woolly had a little lamb,
Little lamb, little lamb,
Woolly had a little lamb,
They found it in the snow.

Poppy brought it home again,
Home again, home again,
Poppy brought it home again,
As fast as she could go.

To listen to the tune of this song, go to the Usborne Quicklinks Website
at **www.usborne-quicklinks.com** and type the keywords "treasury songs".

One, two, three, four, five

(to the traditional tune)

One, two, three, four, five,
Poppy caught a fish alive,
Six, seven, eight, nine, ten,
Then she let it go again.

Why did she let it go?
Because it bit her finger so.
Which finger did it bite?
This little finger on the right!

To listen to the tune of this song, go to the Usborne Quicklinks Website
at **www.usborne-quicklinks.com** and type the keywords "treasury songs".

Naughty Woolly

(to the tune of "Baa, baa, black sheep")

Naughty Woolly,
Trotted through the gate,
Look at all the flowers she ate!

We went to the show and she stood in the ring,
And she won a silver cup, the clever thing!

Clever Woolly,
Running down the lane,
Now let's take her home again.

To listen to the tune of this song, go to the Usborne Quicklinks Website
at **www.usborne-quicklinks.com** and type the keywords "treasury songs".

Dolly, Dollly

(to the tune of "Horsey, horsey")

Dolly, Dolly, don't you stop!
Just let your feet go clippety-clop,
Your tail goes "swish" and the wheels go round,
Giddy-up, we're homeward bound!

The engine's broken, the engine's broken,
So let's go and look for Farmer Dray!
Here comes Dolly, here comes Dolly,
Now we'll soon be on our way, so,

Dolly, Dolly, on your way,
We've got a train to pull today!
Your tail goes "swish" and the wheels go round,
Giddy-up, we're homeward bound!

95

Dolly, Dollly

(to the tune of "Horsey, horsey")

Dolly, Dolly, don't you stop!
Just let your feet go clippety-clop,
Your tail goes "swish" and the wheels go round,
Giddy-up, we're homeward bound!

The engine's broken, the engine's broken,
So let's go and look for Farmer Dray!
Here comes Dolly, here comes Dolly,
Now we'll soon be on our way, so,

Dolly, Dolly, on your way,
We've got a train to pull today!
Your tail goes "swish" and the wheels go round,
Giddy-up, we're homeward bound!

This little piggy

This little piggy went to market,
(Twiddle big toe.)

This little piggy stayed at home,
(Twiddle second toe.)

This little piggy had roast beef,
(Twiddle middle toe.)

This little piggy had none,
(Twiddle fourth toe.)

And this little piggy cried
(Twiddle little toe.)
"Wee wee wee! I can't find my way home!"
(Tickle sole of foot and up to back of knee.)